Fiona Roberton

The PERFECT PRESENT

Hodder
Children's
Books

A division of Hachette Children's Books

For Francis Crumble

First published in 2011 by Penguin Group Australia,
250 Camberwell Road, Camberwell, Vic 3124 Australia

First published in hardback in 2012 by Hodder Children's Books.
First published in paperback in 2013.
Hodder Children's Books is a division of Hachette Children's Books, 338 Euston Road, London, NW1 3BH
An Hachette UK Company

A catalogue record of this book is available from the British Library.

HB ISBN: 9781 444 90894 7
PB ISBN: 978 1 444 90895 4

Printed in China.

www.hachette.co.uk

Chapter 1
The Night Before

Henry was too excited to sleep.

He was thinking about the enormous pile of
birthday presents waiting for him downstairs, and
trying to guess what Spot was going to give him.

He was guessing in alphabetical order and was currently at 'T'.

'Is it a trip for two to Timbuktu?'

'No.'

'A totem pole?'

'No.'

'A trampoline?!'

'No.'

Spot had actually bought Henry a fishing rod.
Whenever they passed the window of Mr Angling's
shop for anglers, Henry would push his nose up
against the window and gaze longingly at it.

CANS
of
WORMZ
DO NOT OPEN ↓

WORMZ

G-ROD T3000 - EL RAYO DE LA MUERTE BLANCO

K. TROUT
FISH
&
TELL
A LIFE

'If only it was mine,' he would sigh.

Spot couldn't wait to see Henry's face when he opened it.

It was going to be the Perfect Present.

Chapter 2
The Surprise

Morning came, and Spot and Henry raced downstairs.

Henry ripped open all of his presents from his mum and dad,

his sister Olivia,

his uncles, aunts and cousins...

...and was just about to open Spot's present...

...when the
doorbell rang.

DING DONG

Henry's grandparents had arrived, and they had brought a strange and wobbling box with them.

They carefully placed it on the floor in front of Henry...

...and with a loud and sudden 'WOOF!' out burst...

'A dog!' yelled Henry. 'With a waggy tail,
a soft wet nose and a warm furry tongue!
He's PERFECT!'

And he ran straight to the garden to
teach the dog some fantastic new tricks.

Spot followed them out into the garden. 'But you haven't opened my present yet,' he said.

But Henry wasn't listening.

Spot was miserable. 'He's always wanted a dog and now he has one,' he thought. 'I might as well not be here.' So he left Henry a note to say goodbye...

...and quietly packed his things.

It was dark outside and had started to rain, but
he shut the door softly behind him, and set off
on the long journey back to his old house.

It was still raining when
Spot came to a river.

His suitcase was too heavy to fly with,
so he jumped in to swim across instead.

But the rain had made
the river too fast
and too strong,

and Spot tumbled
away downstream.

He desperately grabbed at
the branches of a tree as the
river swept him past...

...and clambered unsteadily to the top.
The rain carried on raining and the river rose up to meet him.
Spot was stuck, and didn't know what to do.

Spot had almost given up hope when he suddenly heard
shouting in the distance, and his heart jumped.
Henry had come to find him.

But then he heard barking too, and his heart sank.
The dog was with him. There was a flash of torchlight,
the dog came slowly sniffing over the hill...

...and then barking noisily rushed headlong towards Spot.
'Wait!' shouted Henry, but it was too late.

ROWF!

With a single bound, the dog
jumped into the river...

...and immediately sank like a stone.

Spot knew he had to do something.
He dived straight in after the dog and
caught him by the collar...

...just in time.

But now they were both in trouble.
Spot was too tired and the dog was too
heavy, and they both began to sink.

Then from somewhere up above them there
came a strange 'Ffwwwwiiiiiiiiiiiiiiizzzzz plop',
and Spot felt a sharp tug at his collar.

He looked up, and there was Henry,
holding his brand-new fishing rod and smiling.

'Oh, Spot,' said Henry.
'I was so worried about you.
Why did you leave?'

'Because I didn't think you
needed me anymore,' said Spot.
'I thought the dog was your
Perfect Pet now.'

'Spot,' said Henry. 'I will
always need you, and you
will **always** be my Perfect
Pet, no matter what.'

'But perhaps,' he said, 'the dog can be **our** Perfect Pet? I would never have found you without him.'

Spot looked curiously at the dog. 'I've never had a pet before,' he said.

'You'll love it,' Henry told him. 'Pets are **excellent**.'

'So,' asked Spot hopefully,
'do you like your birthday present?'
'Spot...' replied Henry,

'...it's absolutely perfect.'